Winnie-the-Pooh

and the day of
Very Important Letters

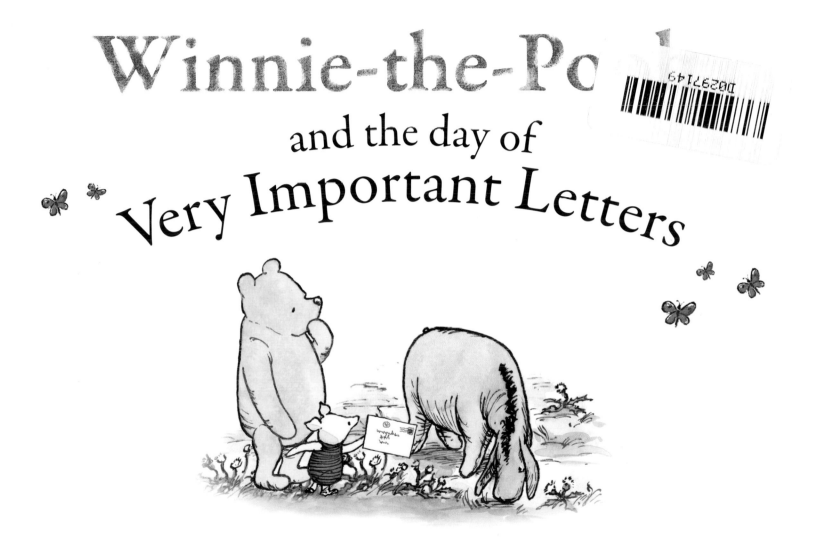

EGMONT

One morning, Piglet's nose was pink with happiness. He had woken up that day and simply known that something exciting was going to happen.

And, sure enough, when Piglet went to his front door to see what kind of day it was (clear and sunny, with drifts of white cloud), there was Pooh standing outside.

"Oh, hello, Pooh," said Piglet. "What are you doing here so early in the morning?"

And Pooh replied, "Hello, Piglet. Well, it is like this, you see," and then he handed Piglet a letter.

And this is what the letter said . . .

Piglet, though, wasn't quite sure what the letter said. And being a Bear of Very Little Brain, Pooh wasn't quite sure what the letter said either.

So they decided to ask Kanga and Roo if they knew anything about the Very Important Letter.

When they arrived, Kanga was showing Baby Roo
how to do little jumps.

"Hello, Kanga," said Pooh. "We've come to tell you about
our Very Important Letter."

But Kanga had received
a letter of her own.

And this is
what it said . . .

"The thing is," said Kanga, "there are some very long words in my letter. I am not sure what it says. I think we should go and see Chrisopher Robin."

Just then, they heard a loud:

Worraworraworraworraworra!

And Tigger bounced into view.

"Hello, Tigger," said Pooh. "We're all off to see Christopher Robin."

And off they all went.

Across the forest, not very far away, Rabbit opened his letterbox and discovered a letter inside.

"Ha!" said Rabbit. "An important letter is just what an important rabbit like me deserves."

And this is what Rabbit's letter said . . .

Rabbit rushed over to Owl's house and showed
his Very Important Letter to Owl.

And wise though Owl was, able to read and spell
his own name (WOL), he somehow went all
to pieces when others watched him.

"Well?" said Rabbit.

"Exactly," said Owl.

"Exactly what?" said Rabbit.

"Exactly what I'd expect a letter to say," said Owl. And he added, "If you hadn't come to see me, I should have come to see you."

"Why?" asked Rabbit.

"Because I received a letter, too," said Owl, seriously.

And he showed his letter to Rabbit.

"How extraordinary," said Rabbit.

"Indeed," squawked Owl. "But the fact is, we still don't know who sent the letters."

And so they decided to visit Christopher Robin, as he was sure to know who had sent them.

Meanwhile, around the same time, Eeyore stood by the side of the stream and gazed at his reflection in the water.

"Nobody cares. Nobody minds," he said, gloomily.

Then Eeyore turned and noticed a letter on the ground.

And this is what his letter said . . .

"How strange," said Eeyore after a while. "The wind must have blown the letter here. And somehow it picked up my name on the way."

Feeling confused, Eeyore ambled off to Christopher Robin's house.

When Eeyore arrived at Christopher Robin's house,
he was surprised to find the other animals there.

"It's like this," explained Piglet, excitedly. "It turns out that
Christopher Robin sent all these letters, but what's really
interesting is that he has one last letter for Someone Very Special."

And when everyone was quiet,
Christopher Robin handed
another envelope to Eeyore.

Eeyore gazed at his envelope, puzzled.
"What does it say?" he said, finally.

So then Christopher Robin opened
the envelope and read aloud the
birthday card that was inside.

"Me, having a real birthday?"
said Eeyore.

"All day long," said Pooh. "Now, I think
you should put on your party hat."

And so everyone sat around a long table, and Eeyore's birthday party began in earnest.

"Eeyore, I do think that party hat suits you rather well," said Pooh.

And Eeyore smiled.